Quahogs
are a
Girl's Best Friend

For Laura

Printed in the United States of America

ISBN 0-924771-50-X

10 9 8 7 6 5 4 3 2

Quahogs
are a
Girl's Best Friend

DON BOUSQUET

Other Books
by

DON BOUSQUET

THE RHODE ISLAND HANDBOOK
(with Mark Patinkin)

THE RHODE ISLAND DICTIONARY
(with Mark Patinkin)

THE QUAHOG STOPS HERE

THE BEST OF THE QUAHOG TRILOGY

DON BOUSQUET'S NEW ENGLAND

I BRAKE FOR QUAHOGS

THE NEW ENGLAND EXPERIENCE

THE QUAHOG WALKS AMONG US

BEWARE OF THE QUAHOG

WELCOME TO THE
OCEAN STATE
PLEASE FEEL FREE
TO PLAY THROUGH
GEE, I LOVE
THIS STATE!
7
DON BOUSQUET

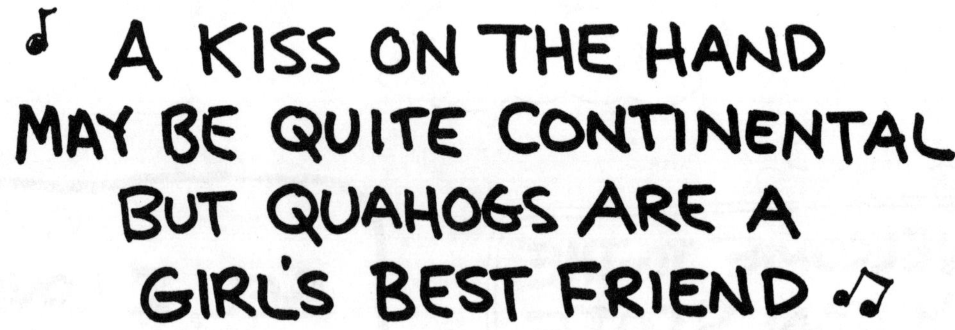
A KISS ON THE HAND
MAY BE QUITE CONTINENTAL
BUT QUAHOGS ARE A
GIRL'S BEST FRIEND
DON BOUSQUET

AIR BAG ADVERTISING

CHANNEL 12
VIEWER, NO DOUBT.
DUMB
AS
EXPLETIVE
DON BOUSQUET

WHERE COFFEE SYRUP COMES FROM

CAPT. KIRK'S BLENDER

TELL THE U.S. POSTAL SERVICE WHICH LIZZIE BORDEN YOU'D LIKE!!

I VOTE FOR:

☐ GOOD LIZZIE ☐ BAD LIZZIE

AS ADVERTISED ON TV !!
THE HAIR CLUB FOR MEN
DON BOUSQUET

SANDPIPERS

GEE, THESE THINGS ARE REALLY UGLY !
DON BOUSQUET

TROLLING
FOR
LAWYERS
DON BOUSQUET

OCEAN STATE
HOME FOR THE
SICK AND TIRED
OF POLITICS
NO VACANCY
DON BOUSQUET

" WE'RE JUST ABOUT THROUGH ALL THAT TURBULENCE, FOLKS AND THERE'S THE BOSTON SKYLINE UP AHEAD... "

"HE'S A COWBOY AND I'M A NATIVE AMERICAN."

SWINDLER'S LIST

INSTANT
QUAKER
RATS
DON BOUSQUET

MERMAID
MERMAN
DON BOUSQUET

LADIES AND GENTLEMEN, WE'LL BE ARRIVING AT PROVIDENCE IN JUST A FEW MIN... WELL, NOT ACTUALLY 'PROVIDENCE'— MORE LIKE WARWICK BUT THEY MAKE US SAY PROVIDENCE BECAUSE THE AIRLINE BELIEVES THAT NOBODY WOULD EVER PAY GOOD MONEY TO GET ON A PLANE WITH A DESTINATION LIKE 'WARWICK'.
DON BOUSQUET

HOMECOMING QUEEN
U.S. NAVALWAR COLLEGE
NEWPORT, R.I.
DON BOUSQUET

FLOSSMORE
BOSTON
DON BOUSQUET

LORD A'MIGHTY, FEEL MY TEMPERATURE RISIN'.... HIGHER AN' HIGHER, IT'S BURNIN' THROUGH TO MY SOUL.... GIRL, GIRL, GIRL YOU GONNA SET ME ON FIRE... MY BRAIN IS FLAMIN' – I DON'T KNOW WHICH WAY TO GO.... YOUR KISSES LIFT ME HIGHER LIKE THE SWEET SONG OF A CHOIR... YOU LIGHT MY MORNIN' SKY WITH BURNIN' LOVE....
I'M JUST A HUNKA HUNKA BURNIN' LOVE I'M JUST A HUNKA HUNKA BURNIN' LOVE I'M JUST A HUNKA HUNKA BURNIN' LOVE I'M JUST A HUNKA HUNKA......
R.I. 6590
DON BOUSQUET

DON BOUSQUET

FOXY LADY
STAGE DOOR
NO ADMITTANCE
NO PARKING
DON BOUSQUET

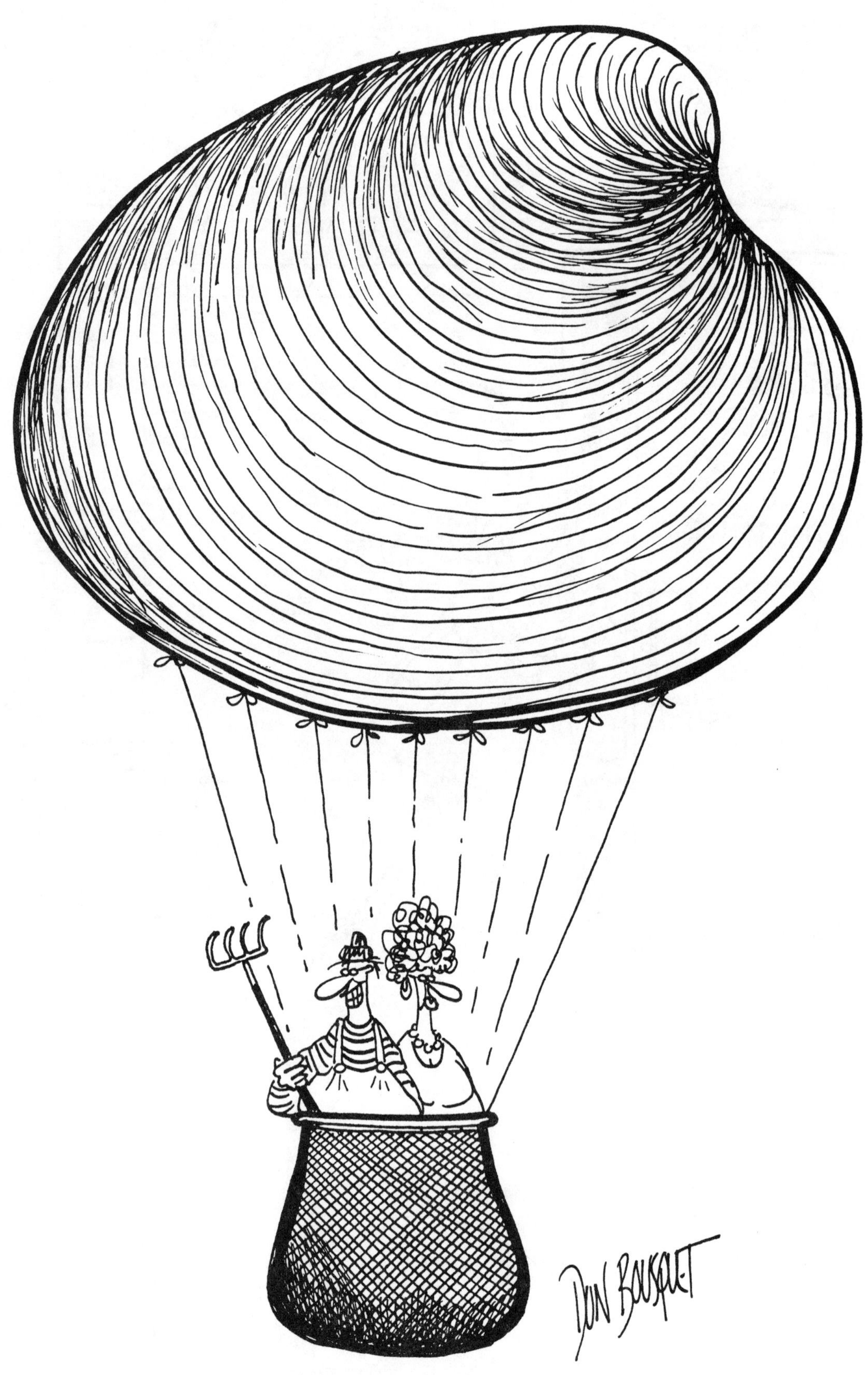
DON BOUSQUET

YOUNG TONY DiBIASIO

DEEP IN THE WOODS OF FOSTER...
...DEVIL(DOG)WORSHIPERS

LUMBERGHINI

JOHNSTON GENETIC ENGINEER
OPENS THEME PARK
FORMER PIG FARMER HOPES
TO ATTRACT HUGE CROWDS
JURASSIC
PORK

" SANTA,.. ABOUT THE TWO FRONT TEETH I GOT LAST CHRISTMAS... "

HUGE TRUCKLOADS OF THESE THINGS, DROPPED FROM THE WORDS OF NATIVE NEW ENGLANDERS, ARE SHIPPED DAILY TO THE MIDWEST WHERE THEY ARE USED ENTHUSIASTICALLY.

SIX WEEKS AFTER BECOMING A BUS MONITOR, DORIS WAS ABLE TO THROW AWAY HER THIGHMASTER DEVICE.
DON BOUSQUET

" IT APPEARS TO BE SOME SORT OF YEAST INFECTION."

"AND ANOTHER THING... NEVER REFER TO THIS PLACE AS THE 'ADULT CORRECTIONAL INSTITUTION.' WE LIKE TO SAY THAT WE'RE ATTENDING THE COMMUNITY COLLEGE OF CRANSTON."

"CHECK OUT THIS GUY IN THE 'BOSTON WHALER'... LET'S HAVE SOME FUN!"

DILITHIUM CRYSTALS
SCOTTY
DON ROUSQUET

"ACTUALLY, I WAS BORN IN CRANSTON BUT I GREW UP IN SOUTH COUNTY..."

OCEAN STATE
HAIR SALON
DON BOUSQUET

" YEAH, THEM BASS WILL GO FOR A FAKE FROG EVERY TIME."

"OKAY, TO GET TO BRISTOL WE HAVE TO GO ACROSS THE JAMESTOWN-VERRAZANO BRIDGE THEN TO NEWPORT OVER THE PELL-VERRAZANO BRIDGE THEN WE GO THROUGH PORTSMOUTH AND OVER THE MOUNT HOPE-VERRAZANO BRIDGE. GOT THAT?"

DON BOUSQUET
"AND YOU FOLKS ON THE RIGHT SIDE OF THE AIRCRAFT SHOULD BE GETTING A REAL GOOD VIEW OF THE BAY ABOUT NOW..."

"THE FORECAST GOES SOMETHING LIKE THIS; A SUNNY START TOMORROW WITH INCREASING CLOUDS UNLESS AN UNKNOWN ASTEROID SIX MILES ACROSS COMES SCREAMING THROUGH THE ATMOSPHERE WITH AN EXPLOSIVE FORCE OF 100 MILLION TONS OF TNT DESTROYING ALL LIFE WITHIN 150 MILES AND CAUSING ...."

WEST WARWICK, R.I. ORDINANCE NO. 31748:
– ALL LICENSED DRIVERS ARE REQUIRED TO CARRY A TRUNKFUL OF COLD PATCH AND A SHOVEL.

" THERE NOW... IS MADAM'S BIB NICE AND SNUG? "

" JUST WAIT 'TIL I GET YOU HOME, MY PRETTY. "

SWAMP YANKEES

GRAND OPENING SALE!

Benny's

SIZZLERS

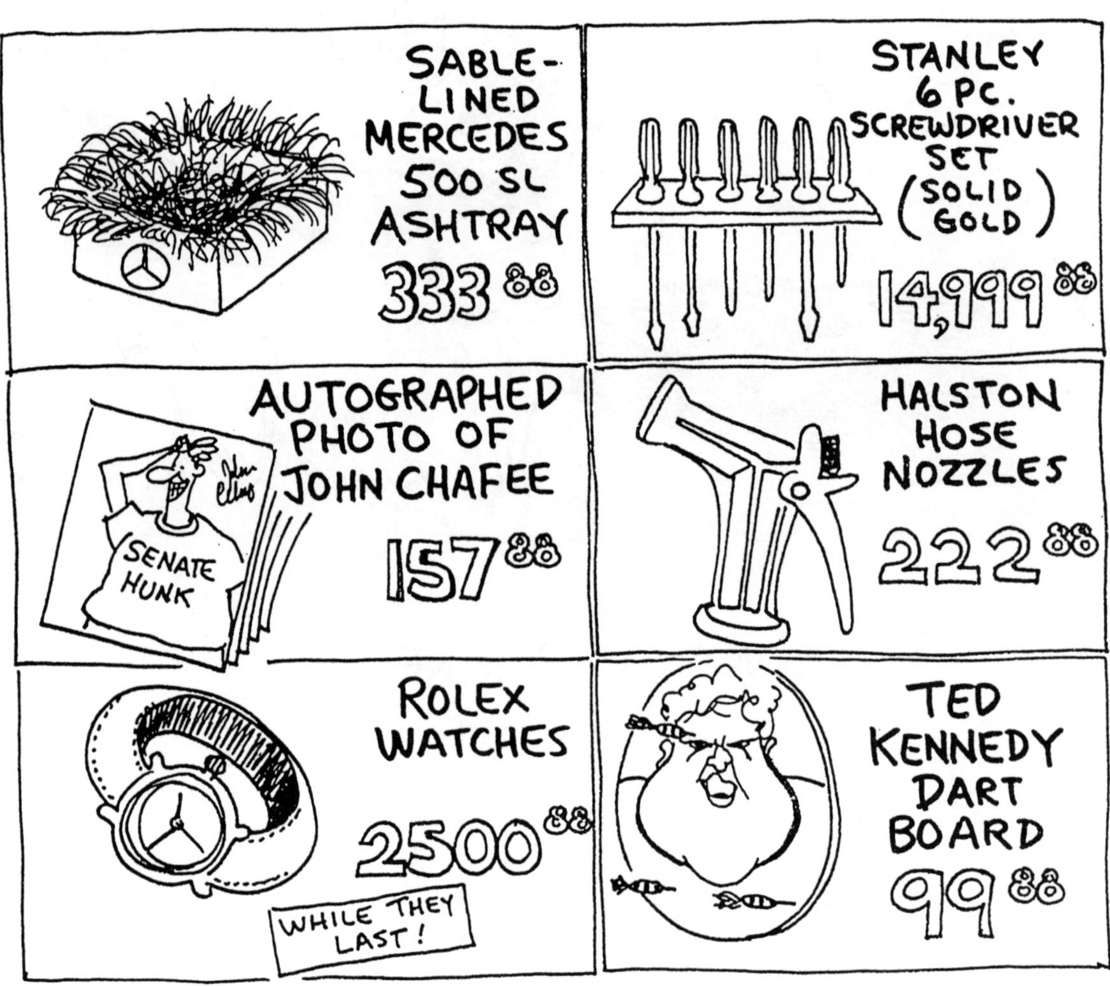

WHEN BENNY'S OPENS A STORE AT WATCH HILL

DON BOUSQUET

FINAL INSPECTION AT THE INJECTION MOLDED QUAHOG DECOY FACTORY, EAST PROVIDENCE, R.I.

DON BOUSQUET

"TAKE IT EASY... I'M HERE FOR YOUR EVINRUDE."

"WE DISCUSSED THIS BEFORE THE OPERATION. WHEN WE GO IN AFTER A REALLY CHRONIC NASAL CRANSTON WHINE, THERE'S JUST NOT A WHOLE LOT LEFT."

IF YOU LISTEN QUIETLY TO PRESIDENT EISENHOWER'S SPEECH, BILLY, MOMMY AND DADDY WILL GIVE YOU ANOTHER BRIGHT AND SHINY ROCK THAT WE FOUND ON SCARBOROUGH BEACH LAST SUMMER.
DON BOUSQUET
RHODE ISLAND IN THE '50's... A SOMEWHAT SIMPLER TIME.

THAT SURE IS A NICE GRIST MILL YOU GOT THERE. IT'D BE A SHAME IF IT GOT BUSTED UP.
YEAH, IF IT GOT BUSTED UP.
EARLY RHODE ISLAND MOB ACTIVITY
DON BOUSQUET

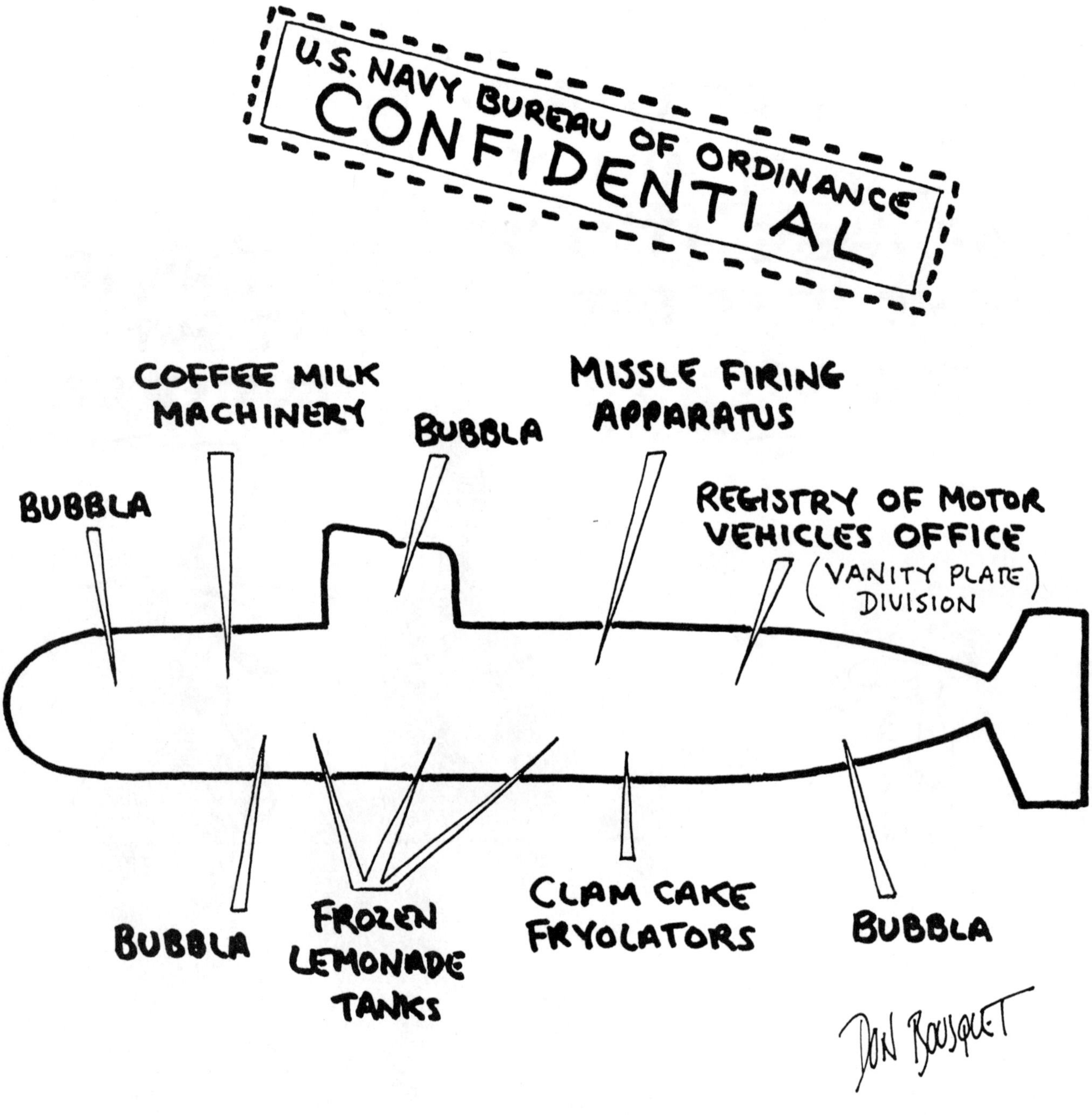

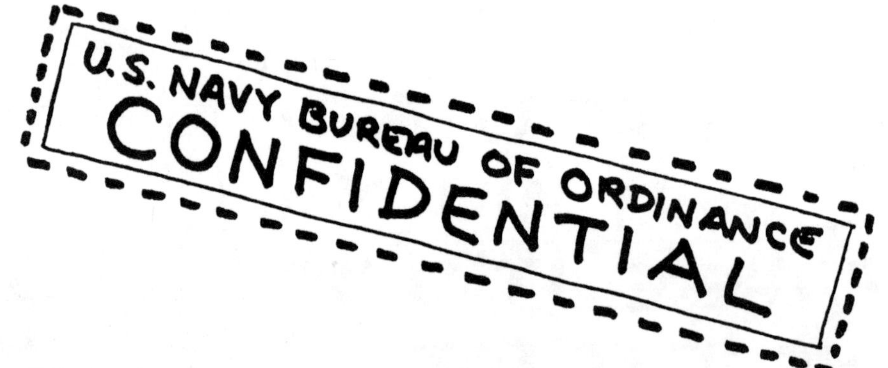

ESSENTIAL EQUIPMENT ABOARD THE TRIDENT SUBMARINE, USS RHODE ISLAND

I CHRISTEN THEE, USS RHODE ISLAND!!
COFFEE SYRUP
DON BOUSQUET

" GEE, IT'S GREAT TO BE BACK IN RHODE ISLAND AGAIN! "

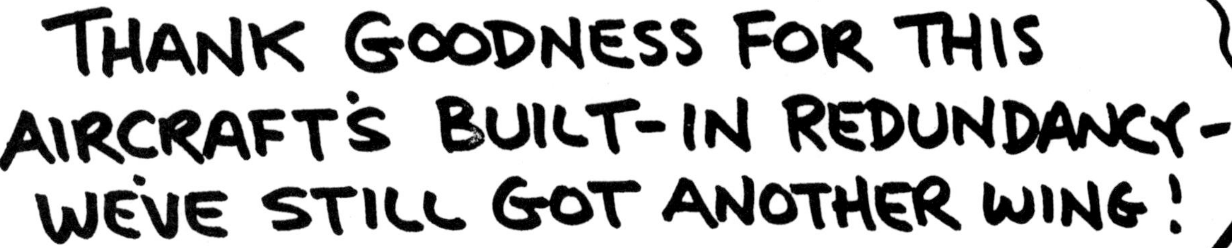
THANK GOODNESS FOR THIS AIRCRAFT'S BUILT-IN REDUNDANCY- WE'VE STILL GOT ANOTHER WING!
DON BOUSQUET

ELECTRIC BOAT HAS ALREADY BEGUN TOOLING-UP FOR THE CIVILIAN MARKET.

UPPER BAY QUAHOGS HAVE BEEN OFF-LIMITS SO LONG THEY'RE GETTING A CHANCE TO EVOLVE.

RHODE ISLAND
STATE OFFICES
DIRECTORY
1ST FL. DIVISION OF TAXATION
2ND FL. DEPT. OF TAXATION
3RD FL. OFFICE OF TAXATION
4TH FL. COUNCIL ON TAXATION
5TH FL. HOUSE OF TAXATION
6TH FL. NIGHT OF THE LIVING TAXATION
DON BOUSQUET

HEADING FOR THE FIRST HOLE

G.O.L.F.

G.RATEFULLY
O.UTDOORS
L.IVING
F.REE

HEADING FOR THE 19TH HOLE

18

G.O.L.F.

DON BOUSQUET

G.IVING
O.FF
L.ETHAL
F.UMES

FLYING BRIDGE

I PUT OUT THE CAT, LOCKED THE DOORS AND SET UP THE SECURITY SYSTEM.
DON BOUSQUET

..FURTHERMORE, THERE WILL BE NOT ANY LISTENING TO THE RADIO OR WATCHING OF THE TELEVISION MACHINE AND NO FANCY CLOTHING OR DANCING OF ANY KIND AND...
AMISH COUNTRY II
DON BOUSQUET

STERN DRIVE

"CAPTAIN'S LOG, STARDATE 4597.3... WE ARE IN ORBIT ABOVE A POLITICALLY VOLATILE, CLASS 'M' PLANET KNOWN AS RHODE ISLAND...

... SPOCK HAS FIRED A FULL SPREAD OF PHOTON TORPEDOES AT THE PLANET'S PRIMITIVE CENTER OF GOVERNMENT. APPARENTLY, SPOCK SAW SOMETHING ON THE SCANNERS TOO HIDEOUS TO BE ALLOWED TO EXIST IN THIS QUADRANT OF THE GALAXY... "

MUMBO JUMBO JET

CHARLESTOWN
EXITS
↑ SLOT MACHINES AHEAD ↑
ROULETTE BEAR RIGHT →
← BLACK JACK LEFT LANES
HOME EQUITY LOANS ALL EXITS
LOANS
DON BOUSQUET

LIKE MOST RHODE ISLANDERS, BOB DOESN'T MIND JUST STAYING HOME ON A SATURDAY NIGHT AND CURLING UP WITH A GOOD BOOK.

"WER'E STILL SHOWING A FOURTEEN BUSHEL SHORTFALL COMPARED TO LAST QUARTER. RAKE FASTER."

" IT CONTAINS HIGH LEVELS OF SLEAZE ENABLING ME TO GRADUALLY WITHDRAW FROM RHODE ISLAND POLITICS."

GARDEN CITY
EXITS
SWEET
CORN
ASPARAGUS
RADISHES
DON BOUSQUET

DON BOUSQUET'S

USED CARS

ECONOMY! 1963 RAMBLER AMERICAN, WHITE, STANDARD SHIFT, NO RADIO, NO HEATER, BLACK WALL TIRES, 5200 MILES. $ 2295.00
CLAIBORNE PELL NEWPORT

LUXO! 1991 LINCOLN STRETCH LIMO, LO MILES, TV, WET BAR, CELLULAR PHONE, LOTS OF LIGHTED VANITY MIRRORS, MIRRORED CEILING, JACUZZI, 3000 WATT STEREO AND P.A. SYSTEM, MUST SELL, NO PLACE TO PARK. V. CIANCI PROVIDENCE

HOT! 1986 PONTIAC TRANS AM, WHITE VELOUR AND LEATHER INTERIOR WITH RHINESTONE STUDDING, NORDIC TRACTION SYSTEM, BACK SEAT CONVERTED TO WEIGHT ROOM AND SAUNA. V. PAZIENZA PROVIDENCE

CLASSIC! 1954 FORD SUNLINER CONVERTIBLE, ONE OWNER, V8, AUTO, NEEDS SOME WORK, TOP WILL NOT GO UP WHEN IT RAINS, AND IT RAINS A LOT, SOMETIMES UNEXPECTEDLY. ART LAKE PROVIDENCE

" PLEASE RETURN YOUR SEAT TO AN UPRIGHT POSITION, MR. LINDBERGH. WE'LL BE LANDING IN PARIS IN JUST ABOUT FIVE MINUTES... "

AFTER A HOSTILE TAKEOVER BY CHANNEL TWELVE

POLITICALLY AND
ANATOMICALLY CORRECT

DON BOUSQUET

THE MATTER WAS FINALLY SETTLED BEFORE A CAPACITY CROWD AT THE CIVIC CENTER

FREE FALL
ROCKY POINT'S
MOST EXCITING
ATTRACTION
ENTER
DON BOUSQUET

NEW ENGLAND
MOB KINGPIN,
VITO SCENARIO

RAJAH WILLIAMS

" YOU WANT SOME FRESH GROUND QUAHOG BITS ON THAT SALAD, PAL? "

DON BOUSQUET

THE WASHDAY MIRACLE

" WE PICKED IT UP AT ONE OF THOSE GIGANTIC ART SALES. YOU KNOW, SOFA SIZE PAINTINGS FOR UNDER TWENTY BUCKS. WE'RE EXTREMELY HAPPY WITH IT."

SLOWLY, NOAH WALKED TO HIS CABIN AS HE REALIZED THE UNICORNS DIDN'T MAKE IT ABOARD BUT TWO LAWYERS DID.

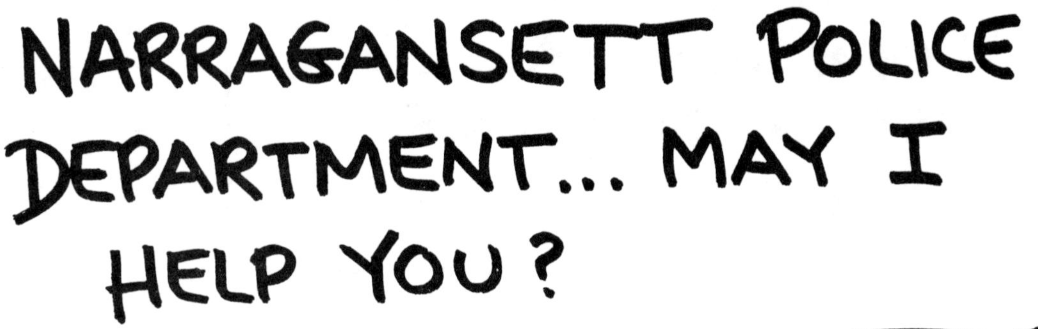
NARRAGANSETT POLICE DEPARTMENT... MAY I HELP YOU?
DON BOUSQUET

EVEN AS A CHILD, 'JOHN FROM ALPERT'S' HAD A DREAM OF IRRITATING THE WORLD

CONVENTION CENTER HOSTS CONFERENCE OF R.I. INDICTED OFFICIALS
HUGE TURNOUT...
DON BOUSQUET

" GO AHEAD... MAKE MY DAY."

TWO DOGS FROM RHODE ISLAND

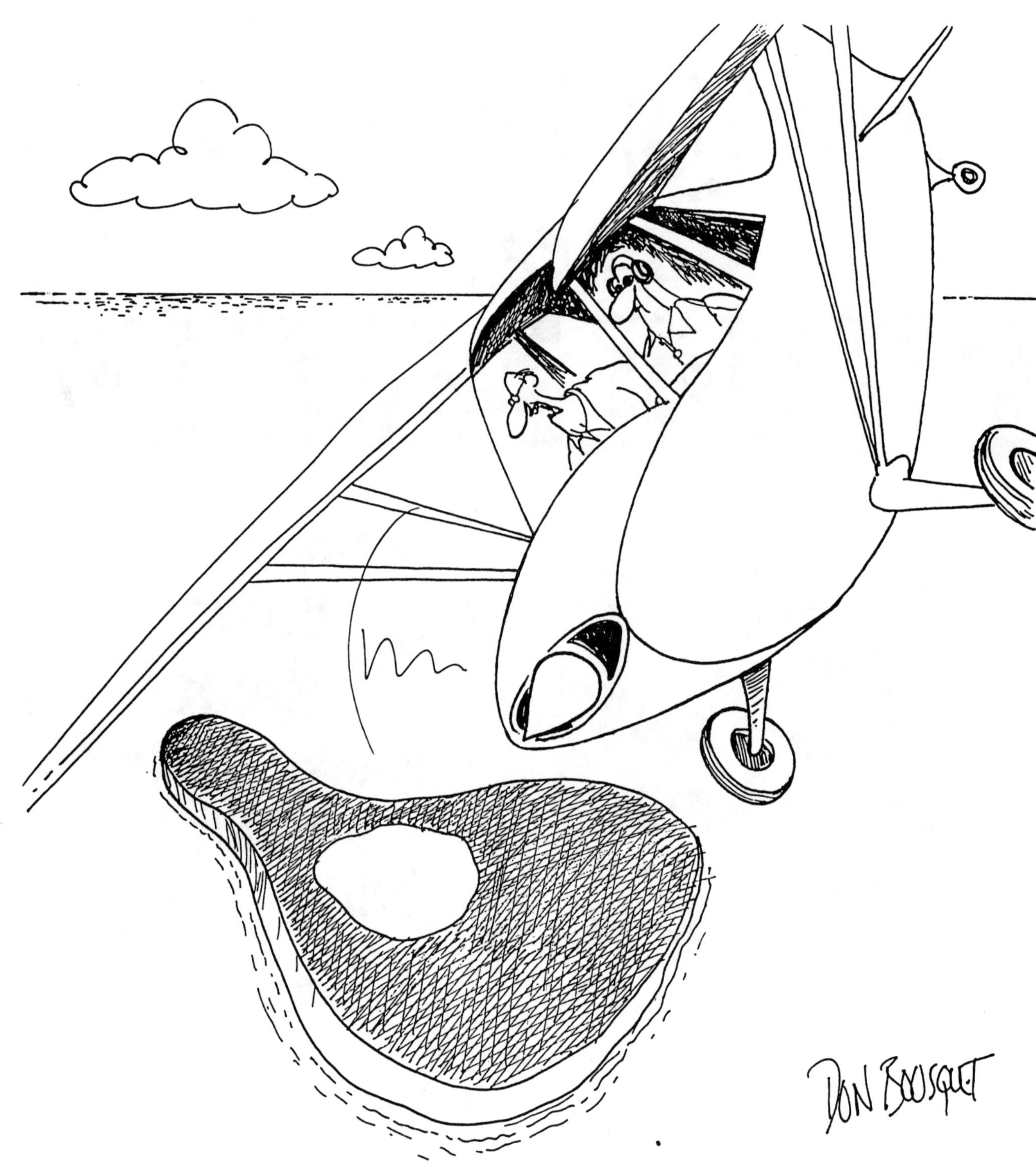

" YOU KNOW, IT'S TRUE... BLOCK ISLAND REALLY IS SHAPED LIKE A PORK CHOP. "

A WALTER BRINE PRODUCTION
SCENT OF A QUAHOGGER
STARRING:
HELD OVER!!

" I JUST INSTALLED A 486 PROCESSOR WITH INTEL OVERDRIVE SUPPORT, FIVE EXPANSION SLOTS, FIVE DRIVE BAYS AND ROOM FOR 64 MB OF RAM. SHE'S GOT A FAX/DATA MODEM, CD-ROM AND TAB-WORKS AND IF YOU BUY NOW I'LL THROW IN A GOOD BULLRAKE."

BORN ON A DIFFERENT ISLAND,
BOB FIT RIGHT IN ON BLOCK.

"YOU SOUND LIKE YOU'RE SIX BRICKS SHORT OF A FULL LOAD, PAL. GOODBYE. NEXT CALLER... LARRY FROM PROVIDENCE, YOU'RE ON THE AIR, AND BY GOD, THIS HAD BETTER BE GOOD."

SOUTH COUNTY PRIORITIES
STAW
LOBSTER TRAP PARTS
AXE HANDLES
LIVESTOCK FEED
12 GAUGE SHELLS
ROAD KILL COOKBOOK
LONG UNDERWEAR
LAG BOLTS
WIFE'S BIRTHDAY PRESENT
OIL FILTER FOR THE TRUCK
TRANSMISSION FLUID
DON BOUSQUET

MISS CENTRAL LANDFILL
AT THE ANNUAL
FOUNDER'S DAY PARADE
JOHNSTON, R.I.
DON BOUSQUET

POPULAR EXHIBITS AT
THE BOSTON CHILDREN'S MUSEUM

CLAMINGOES

COMING SOON –
DISPOSING OF THE OLD JAMESTOWN BRIDGE

ORGANIZING THE A.C.I. CHORUS

NORDIC TRUCK
DON BOUSQUET

RHODE ISLAND
DENTAL WORK
ON A BUDGET

Don Bousquet

NOW BEING TEST-MARKETED
THROUGHOUT THE NORTH EAST

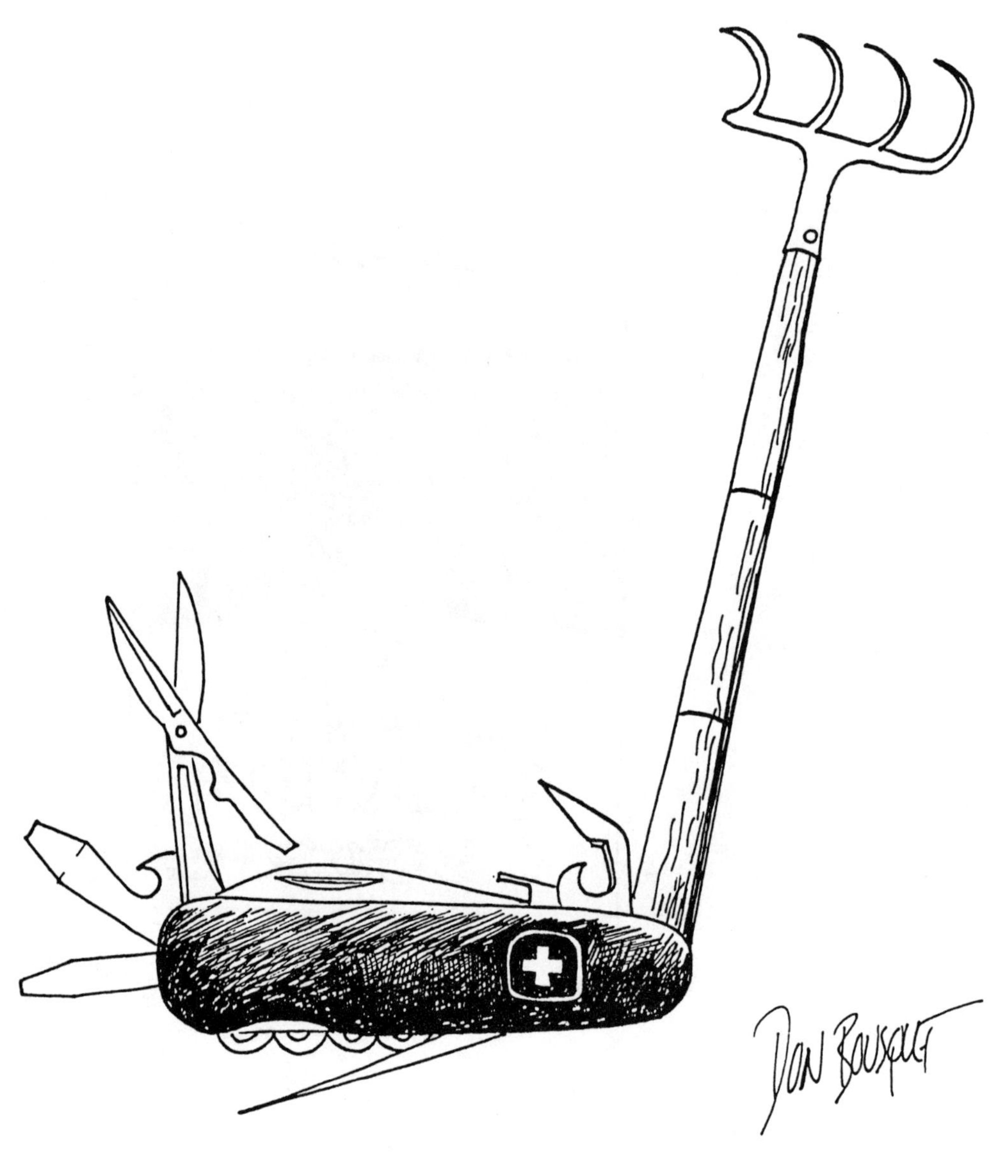

INDISPENSABLE TO THE SERIOUS SHELLFISHERMAN; THE SWISS ARMY RAKE

THE BUDGET OF A NATIVE RHODE ISLANDER

LEAVING THE OCEAN STATE
WOMEN AND CHILDREN FIRST
DON BOUSQUET

NIGHT OF THE WEREHOG
QUICK! GIMME THE SILVER RAKE!
DON BOUSQUET

SAUDI PRINCE BUYS OLD J'TOWN BRIDGE
PAYS STATE $1.5 BILLION
SOLD
WILL RE-ASSEMBLE IN DESERT
MAYOR'S HAIR IS GENUINE
THE NEW YORK TIMES
PROVIDENCE
CLAMCAKES ARE FOUNTAIN OF YOUTH
GALILEE NEUROSURGEON SAYS ALL COULD LIVE LONGER IF ATE 12 DOZ PER
PRESIDENT NAMES NEW DEFENSE SECRETARY
SAYS 'PAZMANIAN DEVIL' IS TOP CHOICE
WASHINGTON
APRIL FOOL
DON BOUSQUET

"I'M SHARON... YOUR USUAL HYGIENIST COULDN'T MAKE IT IN TODAY."

ANIMAL RESCUE LEAGUE
DON BOUSQUET

" YESSIR, JUST LIKE THE AD SAID — SHE'S AN '89 WITH AN ORIGINAL NINE-THOUSAND BLOCK ISLAND MILES."

"ISN'T IT REFRESHING, DOREEN, TO SEE AT LEAST ONE DOCTOR TRYING TO HOLD DOWN THE COST OF HEALTH CARE ?!"

" HEY, KEMO SABE, WE BUY A BIGGER BOAT NEXT YEAR... YOU PADDLE NOW, OKAY ? "

" BUT I DIDN'T ASK WHAT YOUR NET WORTH WAS.... I ASKED WHAT WAS THAT NET WORTH. "

OKAY, I SEE THE BALL.
GIMME MY NUMBER SEVEN
RAKE!

BEAVER AND BOAT HEAD

DON BOUSQUET

WELOME TO THE RHODE ISLAND CONFERENCE OF PUBLIC OFFICIALS WHO HAVE NOT YET BEEN INDICTED FOR ANYTHING
FIRST OFF, I'D LIKE TO THANK YOU ALL FOR ATTENDING...

BACKSTAGE AT WOODSTOCK II

CENTRAL FALLS
COUNTRY CLUB
DON BOUSQUET

LITTLE-KNOWN VILLAGES OF SOUTHERN RHODE ISLAND

DEAR MISS OYL,

WE ARE IN RECEIPT OF YOUR APPLICATION FOR EMPLOYMENT WITH OUR RESTAURANT. THANK YOU FOR YOUR ENCLOSED PHOTO.

ALTHOUGH THERE ARE NO JOB OPENINGS AT THIS TIME, BE ASSURED WE WILL KEEP YOUR APPLICATION ON FILE.

SINCERELY,
PERSONNEL DEPT., HOOTERS, INC.